11/15

LEO & DIANE DILLON

If Kids Ran the World

THE BLUE SKY PRESS

An Imprint of Scholastic Inc. • New York

If kids ran the world,

we would make it a kinder,

better place.

Maybe we'd run the world in a big tree house, and everybody would be welcome.

We'd take care of the most important things.

We know people are hungry,
so all over the world,
everyone would have
enough to eat.

The food would taste delicious, and
it would make people healthy and strong.
Kids who had extra food would help
bring it to people who needed it.

Everyone would have a safe place to live.

Bad housing would be fixed,
and new housing wouldn't
ruin the land or sea.

No matter how sick people were, they would have the medicine they needed.

If you were lonely in a hospital,
kids would come visit you and let
you play with pets.

Somebody friendly
would help you — with a big smile.

Everyone would laugh a lot more.

Kids would have more picnics and games
and funny books and movies.

People would spend more time playing and less
time worrying. No bullying would be allowed.
You could climb trees or dress up
and dance and sing just for fun.

Kids could act very silly.

All children would go to good schools where every teacher was nice and had lots of books, music, and art.

Classes would be exciting and fun.

Schools would serve yummy meals
and have great sports and big playgrounds.

Kids would love school.

People could wear any kind
of clothes, and no one
would tease them.

Children would all live
with people who loved them.

More forests would be planted and protected.

All the beaches, pools, and parks would belong
to everyone. There would be no clubs or places
that kept some people out. Friendship, kindness, and
generosity would be worth more than money.

People would take care of the planet
and animals and plants.

Nobody would throw trash on
the ground or in the ocean
or make the air dirty.

People would have religious freedom, and nobody would punish them or call them names. Everyone would learn the happiness of being thankful.

Even if they were busy, people would remember to stop
to see the beauty of a sunset or a rainbow. All over
the world, people would feel safe with one another.

People would live in
peace together.

No more hate.

Everybody would learn
how to forgive.

If kids ran the world, would these things be possible?
Yes, we think so.

Because kids know that everyone can learn to share.
Kids know how to try to do their very best.

And kids know that the most important thing
in the world isn't money, or being king or queen,
or pushing other people around.

It's love:
giving it, sharing it,
showing it.

And that's why, if kids ran the world,

we'd make it a wonderful place

for everyone to live.

Grown-ups, too.

WHAT KIDS ARE DOING NOW

LIKE OUR FRIENDS in this book, all over the world we are doing things to make our planet a kinder, gentler place. It may not be in the news, but every day, we are making a difference.

What are kids doing?

We volunteer in lots of ways, large and small. Some of us join groups at school or religious organizations, or we volunteer through our communities. We gather food, books, toiletries, and clothing, donating them to shelters or any place they are needed. If we have games or toys or sports equipment we don't use, we give them to someone who will.

Many of us volunteer with our families. It's fun to help build new houses or fix up broken ones so homeless people will have safe places to live. We may sing in a choir and share our songs at hospitals, or teach reading and math to kids who need help at school. Bake sales, car washes, garage sales, babysitting, and dog walking are great ways to raise money. Or we might enjoy coming up with our own ideas, or partnering with friends. A lemonade stand can earn money for people who need help after a tornado, a hurricane, a flood, a fire, or an earthquake.

Some of us volunteer at nursing homes, reading to the elderly or handicapped or blind. Sharing books is so important—and so is supporting teachers and librarians. At animal shelters we do chores and try to find homes for orphaned pets. We clean up trash — at school, on our beaches, in our neighborhoods — and we recycle. We shovel snow, rake leaves, or mow the lawn of a neighbor who can't do it himself, and growing food and flowers in a community garden can be rewarding and fun.

In this book we also talk about some of the ways we treat other people to make them feel good instead of bad. No bullying. Being kind and generous. Not saying hurtful things about our differences. We let people wear their own style of clothes, and follow their own beliefs, and we don't make fun of them. Being friendly and making others feel welcome is good for everyone. We might send a card to a person who is sad or sick, or extend our friendship to the new kid at school. In our playground, everybody is included, and everybody gets a turn at the slide and the swings. We try to laugh more and complain less. We smile. It's easy to be grateful for what we have, and we know how to share.

Across the globe, we are making the world a better place. For birthdays and holidays, some of us give donations instead of store-bought gifts. Grandma's Christmas or Chanukah present might be a five-dollar donation to a homeless shelter, a food bank, or a group that saves lives by providing clean water. Hundreds of worthy organizations are easy to find online or at the library.

Yes, our planet has many problems — so many that addressing them may feel overwhelming and impossible. But even the smallest things we do make a difference. As the old saying goes, "How do you eat an elephant?" The answer: "One bite at a time."

A NOTE TO PARENTS AND TEACHERS

Kids who make the world better will probably grow up into adults who want to do the same thing. Inspiring examples abound. Excerpts from two of President Franklin D. Roosevelt's speeches kept popping up as this book was progressing. The day the text was written, FDR's "Second Bill of Rights" came to our attention. "People who are hungry and out of a job are the stuff dictatorships are made of," he said in a 1944 speech during World War II. So he proposed "a second Bill of Rights under which a new basis of security and prosperity can be established for all—regardless of station, race, or creed." To keep America strong, he advocated the right to a useful, profitable job; decent housing; medical care; and a good education—among other things. "For unless there is security here at home," FDR added, "there cannot be lasting peace in the world." FDR's famous "four essential human freedoms," presented in 1941, are also reflected in this book: Freedom of Speech, Freedom of Worship, Freedom from Want, Freedom from Fear. These basic needs are universal—as is the joy we feel when we feed the hungry, heal the sick, and help the homeless. If peace begins with a smile, then children are our greatest hope for the future.

IN MEMORY OF LEO,
who wasn't able to finish this one.

This book was collaborative. The concept and more than twenty drafts came from our longtime friend and editor, Bonnie Verburg. Despite our protests she chose to be publisher rather than author. We thank her and the multitude of people who work tirelessly to make the world a better place.—L.& D.D.

FDR's Annual Messages to Congress (1944 and 1941) are quoted
from archives of the Franklin D. Roosevelt Presidential Library and Museum.

THE BLUE SKY PRESS

Library of Congress catalog card number: 2013041817
ISBN 978-0-545-44196-4   10 9 8 7 6 5 4 3 2 1   14 15 16 17 18
Printed in Malaysia   108   First printing, September 10, 2014   Designed by Kathleen Westray